My College Crush

Friends to Lovers Series

by

Reba Bale

About This Book

She kissed a girl...and then the girl married a man.

Miranda and Elizabeth were best friends throughout college. They shared everything: the same dorm room, the same group of friends, the same major. Until the night that their friendship became something more, and they shared their first lesbian experience.

The next morning Elizabeth was gone, leaving only a note. She transferred schools and married the "perfect" man her rich parents picked out for her. Other than glimpses in the society pages, Miranda never heard from her again.

Fifteen years later Miranda walks into a Lesbian Spirituality Retreat in the mountains and to her complete shock, one of the other participants is Elizabeth, the woman who broke her heart all those years ago.

Elizabeth spent ten years of her life married to a man she didn't love and keeping up appearances for her controlling parents. When she finally broke away, they disowned her. But now she's living life on her own terms: reading tarot cards, doing yoga, eating vegetarian, and dating women.

Seeing Miranda again is like finding the missing piece of her soul. But after the way she broke her friend's heart, she's going to have to work hard to convince the other woman that she's changed and ready to commit to a long-term love with her college crush.

"My College Crush" is book four in the "Friends to Lovers" romantic novella series. Each book in the series is a steamy standalone featuring an LGBTQ couple making the leap from friends to lovers and looking for their "happily ever after". This book includes explicit sexual activity between consenting adults. It is intended for mature audiences only.

Be sure to check out a free preview of "Spanking Justice: A Middle-Aged Divorcee's First Spanking" at the end of this book!

***

Also by Reba Bale

Affair Recovery
Share Me: A Cheating Husband's Punishment

Dancing with Strangers
Taken by Surprise: A Billionaire Boss Romance

Friends to Lovers
The Divorcee's First Time: A Hot Friends-to-Lovers Lesbian Romance
My BFF's Sister
My Rockstar Assistant
My College Crush
My Fake Girlfriend
My Secret Crush

Paying for Tuition

The Billionaire's Assistant
The Babysitter's Ride Home
The Babysitter's First Ménage
The Teaching Assistant's Lesson

Punishing Holidays
Turkey and a Spanking
Shopping and a Spanking

Sharing With Strangers
The Ride of My Life

Spanking Therapy Clinic
The Reluctant Bride's First Spanking
The Reluctant Bride Gets Caught
The Billionaire Gets Punished
The Curvy Reporter Gets Punished

The Divorce Recovery Team
A Disciplined Budget
Spanking Justice
A Punishing Workout

The Marriage Survival Retreat
Finding His Alpha
Watching His Wife
Exploring His Fantasy

The Voyeur Romance Series
Naughty Dinner Date
Naughty Laundry Day
Naughty Camping
Naughty Love Story
Naughty Sunbathing

Toys for Grown-Ups
Ménage a Geek
Financial Punishment

Unlikely Doms
Alpha in a Sweater Vest
Alpha Student
Alpha Yogi

Standalone

Hotel Spanking
Unlikely Doms
Divorce Recovery Team: A Punishment Experiment Collection
Spicing Up My Marriage
It Takes Three
The Christmas Swap

Want a free book? Join my newsletter and receive a free copy of my book "Hotel Spanking" for free. I promise I will only email you when there are new releases or special sales, so click here[1] and sign up today.

---

1.   *https://bit.ly/rebabooks*

Prologue - Miranda

Fifteen years ago...

"Whoo hoo! My last final is over. O. V. E. R. over."

Elizabeth burst into our dorm room, smiling and talking a mile a minute. She was adorable when she was excited.

I looked up from my laptop and returned her smile. "How'd you do on your test?"

"Aced it, I'm certain."

She flopped into her bed and looked around. "Gosh, this place looks so empty."

It was the end of our junior year at San Francisco University, and we'd already packed up most of our room in preparation for summer vacation. My roommate's family was obscenely wealthy, one of the oldest and most respected families in San Francisco, so her parents had already sent a team to pack and move most of her stuff last weekend.

I had a regular family, which meant I had to pack my shit myself. I didn't really have a lot of stuff here, but I'd still spent a couple of hours packing it up.

When Elizabeth and I had first been assigned roommates freshman year, I'd figured she would be a snob. I'd grown up in southern Oregon, so I didn't know who she was until some of the other girls in our dorm told me about her family.

Everyone in freshman dorm had been surprised that Elizabeth had chosen to go to a state school instead of some fancy Ivy League school, but she'd told me once that she hated all of those "entitled rich bastards" who were in her social circle. Her parents had tried to pressure her into going to a different school, but she had refused to talk to them for a month until they finally relented and agreed to let her go to a "regular" school.

Despite her obvious wealth, Elizabeth was surprisingly down to earth. She wore battered jeans and hoodies, the same as the rest of us, and she didn't flaunt her family's wealth. Honestly, I never would have known she was rich at all if it wasn't for the "staff" that helped her move in and the whispers from other girls on the floor. Well, that and the fancy Mercedes she drove.

Over the last three years Elizabeth and I had become best friends. We shared everything...a dorm room, friends, a major, our dating adventures, and all of our secrets. Well, all of our secrets except one. I was in love with my best friend. And not in a friendly way. It was the one secret I couldn't share with anyone.

Elizabeth knew that I was a lesbian, and while I did my fair share of dating, no one interested me as much as Elizabeth. It was a damn shame, what with her being straight and all. Every time she broke up with a boy she'd tell me, "I wish I was a lesbian, it would be much easier". Little did she know. We pretty much had the same dating problems as heteros.

"So, what's on our agenda tonight?" I asked. "You want to celebrate the end of the school year?"

Elizabeth gave me a huge smile, then opened her backpack. I watched as she pulled out a large bottle of tequila, two shot glasses, a saltshaker wrapped in a baggie, two limes, and a small paring knife.

"Raided the mansion, huh?"

Elizabeth's family home was only thirty minutes away from school, and she regularly went back to get us supplies from the kitchen or the liquor cabinet. She was pretty sure her parents never even noticed that she was there, let alone that she'd swiped anything. Not that they would care if they did. My best friend was the quintessential "poor little rich girl". Her parents only cared about money and appearances, not their incredible daughter. Elizabeth had been raised by a series of nannies, each of whom was clearly a better parent than her own were.

"We're having a pajama party!" Elizabeth announced.

It was one of the things we did to celebrate big events or make each other feel better after a break-up or a bad grade. We'd put on our pajamas, order a pizza, and spend the night sitting on the floor drinking until we couldn't stay awake anymore. Sometimes we'd play cards or give each other manicures, but most of the time we just talked. We had a good circle of friends, but some days we just wanted to have "best friend time", as Elizabeth called it.

Three hours later we were both pretty drunk. We had developed a good tolerance for alcohol over the last three years of school, but get enough tequila in us and we were bound to be silly.

"I'm going to miss you over the summer," Elizabeth slurred, giving me an affectionate smile. "I feel more alive when I'm with you."

I nodded. "Yeah, me too."

Elizabeth scooted over and gave me a side hug. She was always physically affectionate, unlike my own family. They were nice enough and I knew they loved me, even if they didn't say it. In my family, showing your love was more important than talking about it. As a rule, my family wasn't a particularly emotional group. They always told me that I was "the sensitive one in the family" and I guess it was probably true because I'd always been one to wear my heart on my sleeve.

I couldn't complain though. My parents had been super supportive when I came out as a lesbian in high school. Based on stories I'd heard from my other gay and lesbian friends, I know their easy acceptance of my sexual orientation was gift. I didn't take it lightly.

"You're the best thing that's ever happened to me," Elizabeth said, giving me a squeeze. She rested her head on my shoulder and I tried to ignore the shiver of arousal that hit me as I smelled the jasmine scent of her fancy shampoo. My roommate didn't buy shampoo at the dollar store like most of my friends did.

As she snuggled against me, I could feel my nipples hardening under the thin tank top I wore with my sleep shorts. I heard Elizabeth chuckle.

"It's not that cold in here, but mine are doing the same."

Taking that as an invitation to peek, I looked down. Like me, she was rocking full-on headlamps, hers more obvious because her breasts were much larger than mine.

Elizabeth had a classic hourglass figure with large breasts, a thin waist, and rounded hips. She had striking blue eyes that looked lavender in some lights. They shone out brightly against her pale white skin. With her thick and wavy dark brown hair, she reminded me of Elizabeth Taylor in those old movies. She was a stunner, and she got a lot of attention from the boys at our school. And the other lesbians.

I always felt a little plain looking next to her, but I made up for it with my big personality. My sister and I were "mutts", as my mother would say. She was half Native American and half Mexican, and our father was African American, which gave me and my sister a kind of a vaguely ethnic look that seemed to confuse people who wanted to categorize us. People often asked me "What *are* you?" or they would call me "exotic looking".

My hair was straight and dark, my skin was the color of coffee with just the right amount of cream, and my eyes were dark brown. I'd inherited the slimness of my mother's family, where my sister was a little thicker. I was average height with a slim waist, narrow hips, and small breasts. I was completely confident in my body, but I would be lying if I didn't sometimes wish for breasts that filled more than an A cup.

As Elizabeth and I stared at each other's erect nipples, the air seemed to thicken and still. There was this weird energy between us that had never been present before. I dragged my gaze up to look at my best friend's face. Her eyes had darkened, and her breath was coming rapidly between her parted lips.

"Miranda," she whispered, licking her lips, "I..."

Whatever she was going to say, the thought was lost as she surged forward and pressed her lips against mine. I stiffened in shock. Elizabeth was kissing me? What was going on?

I knew that she was really drunk. I told myself I should push her away, but I'd been in love with this woman for three years and I was weak. So weak. Just the touch of her lips made me feel like I was going to burst into flames. When her tongue slid along the seam of my mouth, I had no choice but to let her in. Her tongue swooped in, surprisingly aggressive given I knew for a fact that she'd never kissed another woman before.

Elizabeth pushed me down onto my back, laying on top of me and kissing me like her life depended on it. I could taste the tequila on her breath, and knew my own mouth tasted like our favorite liquor too. My hands rubbed up and down her back and over the sweet curves of her ass. If this was a dream, I never wanted to wake up from it.

When Elizabeth finally broke away, we were both breathless. Our eyes met and held for a long moment. "What are we doing?" I asked, using the last shred of my self-control.

She pressed her finger against my lips. "Shhh..."

She slid down my body, slowly and sensuously. She wiggled until I spread my legs, allowing her access to shove her luscious hips between my thighs. Reaching up, she shoved my tank top up to my armpits, baring my small breasts. Being roommates, I know she'd seen my breasts before, but still she inhaled deeply and whispered, "Beautiful."

She lowered her head and took one of my breasts into her mouth, circling my nipple with her eager tongue. I gasped. It felt so good. Elizabeth bit down softly, and the jolt of pain shot straight to my pussy. I lay there, helpless to stop this, as she gave the other nipple the same attention.

Elizabeth kissed her way down my abdomen before rising onto her knees so she could tug off my sleep shorts and panties. Lowering herself onto her stomach, she bent my knees up and out to the side, opening me even wider. She made a moaning noise as she stared at my glistening pussy. Her eyes were filled with hot lust.

I pushed myself up onto my elbows as caution rang in my brain once more. "Elizabeth. What are you doing?"

She looked up from her inspection of my pussy. "What I've wanted to do for three years."

She lowered her head and licked me from bottom to top. I squirmed beneath her, and she clamped her hands on my hips with surprising strength, holding me still. She licked up and down, alternating between soft slow licks and rougher deeper ones. When I was trembling beneath her, she shifted and inserted one long finger into my dripping channel.

She began fucking me with her finger roughly while she tapped at my clit with her surprisingly talented tongue.

"I'm close," I finally gasped. "Oh my god, I'm going to come!"

She redoubled her efforts, adding a second finger while sucking my swollen clit into her mouth. She closed her lips around me, and I lost the last thread of my control. I wailed her name as my orgasm raced down my spine, making me stiffen and jolt underneath her surprisingly talented tongue.

I came longer and harder than I ever had in my life.

When the waves of my orgasm finally slowed, she shifted forward and rested her chin on my lower belly.

"You look beautiful when you come," she whispered, awe in her voice. "Now do me."

When I woke up the next morning she was gone. I never saw her again.

Miranda

I took a deep breath as I pulled my battered blue Subaru into the parking lot at the Sagebrush Hot Springs Retreat Center. The summer air coming through my window was fresh and fragrant, a nice change from the city. I'd come to this Retreat Center in the Oregon mountains to attend a lesbian spirituality retreat. After nearly two years without a vacation, I couldn't be more excited to have a whole weekend in the woods to relax and recharge.

I parked in the gravel parking and looked around. I'd been to Sagebrush many times over the years, and I always loved it. The Retreat Center was pretty rustic. Guest stayed in one-room log cabins and used separate communal bathhouses. In the center of the property there was a large, historic lodge where communal meals and classes were held.

Sagebrush was completely surrounded by nature, with old growth forest on three sides and a wide and fast-moving river on the other that the Retreat Center used to generate hydroelectric power.

The best part, of course, were the hot springs that were scattered around the property. The naturally occurring hot springs were nestled between the trees that ringed the property. Over the years the cooperative community that ran the Retreat Center and served as stewards of the land had added steps and platforms around many of the pools to make them more accessible to visitors. Soaking in the mineral-enriched hot water was always a special treat.

Sagebrush was where the last of the hippies lived, and it was super popular as a place where lesbians could visit and get back to nature.

I checked in at the small cabin that served as the reception office, then brought my supplies to the one room cabin that was assigned to me. It was simple with a double bed, a small closet, and a table and chair that looked out towards the woods behind the cabin. The cabin was lit by one lamp, and there were no electrical outlets, as a way for the Retreat Center to save electricity.

The bathhouse assigned to my row was a few cabins up the "road", the dirt path that separated the buildings. I popped over to pee and store my toiletries, then returned to my cabin to unpack the meager belongs I'd brought with me. I rolled out my sleeping bag on the bed, remembering that even in summer these cabins tended to be chilly at night. I turned off my cell phone and stored it in my backpack. There was no service up here, and even if there was, I was here to disconnect for the weekend.

It was Friday, and our opening session for the retreat was happening in half an hour so I needed to get ready.

I'd meant to get up here earlier, but I'd run into traffic leaving downtown Portland where I worked as a social worker at a center for homeless youth. It didn't pay very well, but I lived simply and was grateful I could use my degree to help kids who didn't have any place to go. The fact that such a high percentage of them identified as LBGTQ made the work even more personal for me. Not every kid parents who were supportive of their sexual orientation, the way my family was.

I quickly changed out of my jeans and into fitted yoga pants, an old Melissa Etheridge concert tee, and a zip front hoodie from work. I knew we'd be doing some yoga and meditation and I wanted to be comfortable. I stuffed a notebook, pen, my stainless steel water bottle, and a flashlight into a tote bag. I knew from experience that it got very dark here at night, given that there were no outside lights. Taking one last look around my tiny cabin to make sure I hadn't missed something, I headed down the path to the lodge.

I stopped in the dining room to fill up my water bottle and took a long swig of the fresh clear water. This high in the mountains, the water came right from the snow cap. It was delicious.

Making my way to the so-called "Great Room" of the Main Lodge, I checked in with the friendly woman sitting at the table by the door. She gave me a little bag full of stuff for the retreat. I stepped away and peered inside. A name tag. A pen. Another notebook. A folder that included our schedule for the weekend and several other handouts. A battery operated candle. An eye bag that smelled of lavender. Wow, nice swag.

I used one of the markers on a side table to write my name on the name tag, then slipped it into the plastic sleeve and attached it to my shirt with the little magnets that held it in place. I looked around, seeing about twenty other women milling around of different ages. I was glad to see that there were a few other people of color in attendance; I hated being the only non-white person in a group.

Meditation cushions were arranged on the floor in a large circle. Picking a cushion at random, I kicked off my shoes lowered myself to the floor. The buckwheat cushion was surprisingly comfortable. I pulled out the folder with the schedule to look over the handouts and get a better idea of the plan for the weekend. While I was reading, someone sat down next to me, and I looked up with a smile. My eyes widened in shock.

The woman next to me was the spitting image of my former best friend and first love, Elizabeth. It couldn't be, could it? This was the last place I would expect to see her. But the woman had the same thick dark hair, and blue eyes that almost looked violet. She even had the same little birthmark under her right ear.

She was dressed in leggings, wool socks, and a tie dyed t-shirt. The woman's head cocked to the side, one thick braid sliding down her shoulder as she looked at my face, then my name tag, then my face again.

"Miranda?" she gasped, her tone surprised. "Oh my God! Is it really you?"

Before I could answer her question, she pushed herself up to her knees and pulled me into a warm hug. I remained stiff in her arms. What was happening?

"I missed you, Miranda," she whispered into my ear, as if we'd just returned from summer break instead of running into each other after fifteen years. She hugged me like it hadn't been fifteen years since she broke my heart, then left in the night like a thief, with only a note and my memories to remember her by.

I was shocked. I was furious. I opened my mouth to say something, anything, but just then the facilitator rang a gong from the center of the circle, calling our attention to her.

"Good evening. Let's get started."

Elizabeth

I wanted to talk to Miranda, but the retreat was starting. The facilitator asked us to bow our heads, close our eyes, and focus on the movement of our breath. I couldn't concentrate on anything else but my breath. It was coming in short, rapid bursts as I tried not to hyperventilate.

Miranda Williams. The only person I'd ever truly loved. I'd long since given up on ever seeing her again, but now here she was sitting next to me at this remote lodge in the Oregon mountains. What were the chances?

As the facilitator led us through a guided meditation, her voice soft and calm, I let my mind wander. Although I didn't realize it at the time, I had fallen in love with Miranda the moment I saw her freshman year of college. After a huge battle with my parents, they'd given me permission to live on campus instead of driving back and forth to class every day. We only lived thirty minutes away from the university, but I wanted to have a typical college experience.

Miranda and I had been randomly assigned to be roommates based on a compatibility survey we'd filled out. She'd strutted into our room with nothing more than two large duffel bags and the clothes on her back. Walking into our dorm room for the first time, she had looked around and raised her eyebrows.

"How much crap do you have?"

I knew then that we would be best friends. I didn't know we'd be so much more.

My parents had sent the housekeeper and their gardener to help me move into the dorm. Although I'd carefully kept things on my side of the room, I had to admit that I'd probably brought too much stuff. I hadn't realized our room would be so small. The entire dorm room was the size of my en-suite bathroom at home. Living in a dorm had been an adjustment, but I'd loved living in a community and just being one of the girls.

Despite our differences, Miranda and I became fast friends. Unlike the kids in my high school, she didn't care about my money or my family name. Being from a middle class family in Oregon, none of that was important to her. My friend judged people on their actions, not the size of their wallets.

She'd told me on that very first day that she was a lesbian, worried that I might be homophobic or something. I didn't know any other lesbians, or if I did I wasn't aware of it, but her sexual orientation didn't bother me. Unlike my uber judgmental parents, I tried really hard to be open minded.

Everything had been perfect between us until the last day of junior year. We'd gotten super drunk, and with the loss of my inhibitions, I had finally acted on the feelings I'd been having for Miranda. Somewhere along the way my feelings of friendship had turned to straight out lust. I dreamed about her at night, and when I was alone in our room I would touch myself and imagine it was her fingers making me come instead of my own.

Then one night, that dream came true.

I knew instinctively that Miranda was attracted to me, but I also knew that she would never act on any attraction she felt. With the help of my friend tequila, I screwed up my courage and kissed her. And then I did more. The minute my lips touched her wet pussy, I realized that I was not quite as straight as I'd always imagined. When Miranda made me come harder than I'd ever come in my life, that suspicion was confirmed, although I'd tried to deny it for many years.

After we made love, we'd fallen asleep in each other's arms. I think we both probably figured it was the start of something special. Until I woke up, sober and full of regrets.

I'd looked at Miranda's naked body spread out on the bed next to mine and freaked out. What had I done? I was a Hamilton. Hamiltons did not have same sex relationships, or anything else that would cause a scandal.

Had I just ruined my relationship with my best friend? Even at that young age, I understood that my actions the night before would fundamentally change our friendship. I'd slid out of bed, trying hard not to hyperventilate. I was so confused.

Was I a lesbian? Was I bi? What I felt for Miranda didn't just feel like a drunken experiment. Just then my phone beeped with a message from my mother.

We're having dinner with the Rutherfords tonight. Jane and I think that you and Michael would make a good couple. Please dress appropriately and be home by six.

As much as I tried to imagine telling my parents that I was in love with Miranda, I was a coward. I was only twenty, and I couldn't imagine defying my parents and their expectations to be in a lesbian relationship. No doubt they would cut me off from their financial support, and then what would I do? My parents had always been clear that when the time came, I was expected to marry someone "of the appropriate social stature". Even if my parents had been open to my being a lesbian, there would be no way they would accept a mixed race low-income girl from rural Oregon.

And so, I'd taken the coward's way out. I'd scribbled a note to Miranda, gathered up the rest of my stuff, and snuck out of our room like a thief while she was still sleeping. I returned home to my parents and moved back into my childhood bedroom. That night I had dinner with Michael Rutherford and our parents. He was boring as fuck, and I wasn't even a little bit attracted to him, but he was nice enough, and I knew he met my parents requirements for a mate.

When my mother strongly suggested that I transfer to Stanford to be closer to Michael I'd agreed. There'd been no way I could stay at the same school as Miranda, seeing her every day, knowing I couldn't be with the woman I loved.

Twenty year old me was a conflict avoidant chickenshit. Thirty five year old me was a completely different person. Thank God. If I could get Miranda to give me another chance, I would not make the same mistake as I had all those years ago.

I looked at Miranda out of the corner of my eye. The years had been good to her. Her hair was a little bit longer than it used to be. But other than the fine lines around her eyes, she still looked like the twenty year old beauty I'd fallen in love with.

I'd come to this retreat hoping to reconnect with my spiritual side. Little did I know that the universe had a different kind of reconnection in mind for me. I believed in fate. It was no accident that Miranda was here, and I fully intended to take advantage of the gift of getting a second chance to make things right.

I just needed to convince her.

Miranda

It was impossible for me to concentrate on the retreat with Elizabeth sitting next to me. Seeing her had rocked my quiet little world. What was she doing here, at a lesbian spirituality retreat of all places? Last I'd heard she'd married some rich white guy and gone off to live happily ever in the land of the wealthy.

I studied her covertly. She pretty much looked like everyone else here: hippie lesbian. Her clothes were old and comfortable looking with no designer label in sight. The Elizabeth I knew as a kid would never meditate or write in a journal. That kind of stuff was "too weird" for her. And she certainly would never be caught dead at a lesbian event. Appearances meant everything to her parents, and as free-spirited and easy going as she'd tried to be in college, she'd never forgotten that her family was in the spotlight in San Francisco.

The opening session finally ended just in time for us to head into the dining room for dinner. The Retreat Center served a delicious menu of vegetarian food, mostly grown on site by the year-round residents. I'd been looking forward to the incredible Sagebrush food ever since I decided to come.

I pushed myself up to standing, ignoring Elizabeth calling my name, and followed the rest of the group into the dining room. After filling my plate, I settled at a table near the window where I could people watch. Sagebrush attracted the most fascinating collection of lesbians, aging hippies, and young hipsters who liked to get back to nature. The retreat center was unspoiled and comforting. The rustic conditions and vegetarian food here were not going to work for anyone looking for a fancy resort.

I felt Elizabeth's presence before I saw her. She slid her tray onto the table across from me and sat her happy ass down as if we were still friends.

"Hey," she said, giving me a tentative smile. "May I join you?"

"I'd really rather you sat somewhere else," I replied even though I knew her well enough to know that her question had been rhetorical. She'd always been stubborn as hell. If she wanted to sit here, she would. Sure enough, she didn't move away despite my cold words.

"How have you been?" she asked, as if we were casual acquaintances who'd run into each other at the grocery store. She took a bite of her lentil loaf and gave a little moan of pleasure.

"Are we really going to do this?" I asked, my voice cold.

Elizabeth sighed and set her fork down. "I'm divorced now."

I looked up and met her violet eyes, knowing immediately that it was a huge mistake. I felt an immediate rush of attraction for her, and I cursed my fickle body. How was it possible that she was even more beautiful than she had been fifteen years ago? I'd thought I'd gotten over what had happened with Elizabeth. I hadn't thought about her in years, but seeing her here was bringing everything rushing back to the surface again.

"Congratulations."

"I tried it their way. My parents I mean," she started. "I gave it my best shot, but that wasn't the life for me."

I ignored her and shoveled food into my mouth. I'm sure it was delicious as always, but I couldn't even say what I was eating. I was too distracted by Elizabeth to enjoy it. Yet another thing she had ruined for me.

"I graduated from Stanford, got married, bought a house, became a happy housewife, and went to those same fancy ass events that my parents attended," she continued, her tone contemplative. "I kept telling myself, Elizabeth, what you felt for Miranda was just a phase, an experiment. It wasn't really romantic love, so forget about it."

My head shot up. I wasn't aware that she'd felt anything for me, other than drunken lust.

"I could scarcely stand to have my husband touch me. I told myself it was because he was bad in bed, or maybe I was frigid like he'd always told me I was. Then one day I realized that the only time I'd ever had an orgasm that wasn't self-administered was with you."

"Poor baby."

She gave me a disapproving frown, but continued. "Then about five years ago I walked out of my Pilates class, and I saw this woman running on the treadmill. Sweat was dripping down her chest, and her tits were bouncing underneath the sports bra she was wearing as a shirt. I felt this immediate rush of arousal, and then it hit me. I'm a lesbian. I felt more lust for that woman on the treadmill than I'd felt for any man, ever. The problem wasn't that I was frigid or even that my husband was a bad lover, the problem was that I was living a lie. I'd built my entire life around the lie that I was straight."

I stared at her while she took a few bites of her food.

"Gosh, this is delicious," she mumbled. "I've never been here before but I'd always heard the food was incredible."

I raised my eyebrows, silently willing her to continue her story.

"That same day I went home and told Michael that I wanted a divorce. He was shocked. I guess he thought everything was fine with us, and I guess I couldn't blame him, it wasn't like I'd expressed my unhappiness to him. When I told my parents, they freaked out more than my husband did. When I told them that I was a lesbian they disowned me. No surprise there."

"And the treadmill woman?" I couldn't help but ask.

"My first lesbian relationship," she confirmed. "We were only together for about six months, but I learned a lot about myself during that time. I'm grateful to her, even though it didn't work out."

I nodded. I couldn't decide how I felt about this story, but I was crystal clear on the shot of jealousy that hit me as I thought about this other woman being with Elizabeth.

"Do you still live in Oregon?" she asked, seemingly oblivious to my internal turmoil. "Did you go into social work like you'd planned?"

"Yeah, I live in Portland now though. I work at a drop-in center for homeless youth. What about you?"

"I'm living in Seattle now. I'm a tarot card reader and an artist. I sell goddess-themed paintings and art prints at fairs and a couple of new age shops."

I choked on my quinoa. That was literally the last career I would have imagined for her, other than maybe longshoreman. Elizabeth had always hated fish.

"Are you fucking with me?"

"Nope." She opened the huge cloth bag that she'd set on the chair next to her and pulled out a deck of tarot cards. "Maybe I can do a reading for you later."

"Jesus Christ," I said, staring at the well-worn deck of cards in her hand. "Who are you?"

"The one who let you get away," she said, her voice more serious than I'd ever heard it. "I'm not going to make that mistake again."

Elizabeth

Miranda's mouth dropped open. She stared at me incredulously. "What are you saying?"

"I'm saying that I'm in love with you." My words were filled with the conviction that I felt down to my soul. I'd known the minute our eyes connected earlier. The truth me like a bolt of lightning; I'd been in love with Miranda fifteen years ago and absolutely nothing had changed.

"In love with me? Are you nuts? We don't even know each other."

I brushed my hand in the air dismissively. "We know each other. We just need to catch up on the last fifteen years."

I leaned forward and bit my lip. "I tried to look you up a couple of times," I admitted. "I didn't know where you'd gone after college. You changed your phone number, and your social media is all set to private."

"I'm sorry I made it hard for you to cyber stalk me," she said sarcastically.

The Miranda I'd known in college was never sarcastic. I wondered if this was part of her personality now, or if it was just put on for me. I didn't blame her for hating me. I'd hurt her deeply. I wasn't naïve. I'd always suspected that she had feelings for me in college. That was why I'd felt confident kissing her, knowing I wouldn't be rebuffed. What I hadn't fully expected was the depth of my feelings for her.

I knew it was shitty of me to leave her a note and sneak out like that after our incredible night together. I couldn't bear to face her, to tell her that I was too much of a coward to accept the love she offered so freely. I'd tried to write to her a couple of times our senior year, trying to apologize, but my letters were returned unopened. I'd fucked up big time, but I was getting a second chance now, and I wasn't going to waste it.

"Are you married? Seeing anyone?" I asked.

"I don't know how that's any of your business," she grumbled. Her answer and the way she avoided my eyes told me she was single. She always got shifty eyes when she was avoiding something.

"Miranda."

My voice was firm and serious, and her head snapped up to meet my gaze. Another thing I'd discovered since I'd come out as a lesbian: I had a little bit of a dominant side. I felt a rush of dampness flood my panties as I imagined tying Miranda to a bed and licking every inch of her body until she was begging me to let her come.

"When I read my tarot cards last week, the cards indicated that I would be reunited with someone from my past. I thought maybe I'd run into an old girlfriend or someone from school, or maybe even hear from my parents. But now I know what the cards were trying to tell me. The universe is giving us a second chance, so I want to be crystal clear about my intentions here. I don't care how long it takes to prove myself to you. Unless you're already married, you will be mine."

Miranda shot out of her seat like she'd been jolted with a live wire.

"You have a lot of nerve," she hissed angrily. "I've been looking forward to this retreat for months. You will not ruin it for me. I don't know what game you think you're playing, but you had your chance with me. You had your chance and you snuck out rather than facing me. You freaking moved to another school to avoid me. You heard me Elizabeth, more than anyone else ever has, and I can't forget that. Us running into each other here means nothing."

I felt a jolt of pain as she added, "You mean nothing to me. Leave. Me. Alone."

I watched her race off and tried not to cry. Over the years I'd learned to trust that the universe would provide for me. I'd learned to trust my gut. And my gut told me that I should follow her.

Grabbing my bag, I took off in the direction that Miranda had gone. She was headed towards the cabins, practically running through the trees. I followed at a dead run, catching up with her just as she reached the door of her little cabin. I grabbed her arm and turned her to face me. Both of us were breathing heavily but I knew it was from the emotions more than the short jog.

"What?" she gasped. "What do you want now?"

"You."

Before she could respond, I crashed into her with my lips. She stood stiffly for a long painful moment. I nipped at her bottom lip, and she relaxed with a sigh. I took advantage, shoving my tongue into the sweetness of her mouth, sliding it along hers.

She dropped her bag and wrapped her arms around my waist. Before I realized what was happening, she turned me around and pressed me against the door of her cabin, pressing her body into mine. Miranda took over the kiss, plundering my mouth and gripping my ass with her fingers so tightly I was sure I'd have bruises.

Maybe Miranda had discovered a bit of a dominant side too.

If I'd had any doubts that what I'd felt for Miranda in college was just infatuation, those doubts evaporated. In Miranda's strong embrace I felt whole for the first time since college. My entire body felt like it was on fire, yet my mind had never felt calmer.

I threaded my fingers through the sleek strands of her hair, holding her close to me, and she responded by snaking one hand between us and pinching my nipple. Hard. I gasped even as moisture flooded my panties. My God, how had I given her up? I would regret abandoning Miranda until my dying day. I sent a silent prayer to the goddess promising to not squander this second chance.

Miranda tweaked one nipple, and then the other, and rolled her pelvis roughly against mine. I moaned against her mouth, and it seemed to break her out of our haze of arousal. She stepped back, wiping her mouth with her hand.

"That can't happen again," she whispered, her voice unsteady. I wasn't sure which one of us she was trying to convince.

I decided a strategic retreat was in order. I stepped around her to the dirt path. She stayed in place, staring at the door to her cabin.

"It's going to happen again Miranda. And soon. Sleep well."

Then I walked away.

Miranda

I'd expected a sleepless night after everything that had happened with Elizabeth, but to my shock I'd fallen into a deep dreamless sleep almost the minute my head hit the pillow. I awoke with the sun, surprisingly refreshed.

I headed to the communal bath house so I could pee, brush my teeth, and take a shower. When I got back, I changed into capri length tights, a flannel shirt over a tank top, and thick wool socks. Shoving my feet into hiking boots, I grabbed my bag and headed to the lodge.

Breakfast was steel cut oats with a variety of toppings, gluten free muffins, and herbal tea. The only bad thing about Sagebrush was that they eschewed caffeine. It was something about not wanting to pollute the body. I'd meant to bring coffee and a French press that I could use in my room, but I had left it on the counter at home. Oh well, I guess I was going to cold off caffeine cold turkey this weekend.

After I ate my breakfast, I headed back to the meeting room. After settling onto a cushion in the retreat center, I reviewed the day's agenda. I was the first person there, so I was completely unsurprised when Elizabeth joined me a few minutes later. She lowered herself down onto a cushion to my right, moving with a natural grace that I'd always admired.

"Good morning," she said brightly. She was dressed in a black broomstick skirt and a long, light blue sweater. Beads and crystals adorned her neck and both wrists. She looked very witchy. It was a good look for her.

I nodded but didn't respond. Maybe if I ignored her she'd go away?

She pulled out a large travel mug and sighed happily as she took a sip. "Coffee?"

That got my attention. I turned to look at her, then whispered, "You brought contraband?"

She gave me a mischievous smile. "You do NOT want to see me without caffeine."

"I remember." I accepted the mug and took a large sip of the cold brewed coffee. It was delicious. "Yum."

"Seattle is the coffee capital of America," she told me. "I've gotten very discerning about my coffee choices."

We settled in for a morning of yoga, meditation, journaling, and discussion. I was pleasantly surprised at how into this Elizabeth was. The Elizabeth I once knew would have never talked about manifesting or the energy fields of the Earth, or anything she deemed "woo woo".

After a group lunch with all the retreat participants, the facilitator announced that we would be doing a solo walking meditation. It was a nice day, and the walking meditation would be a good way for us to keep our energy up and avoid the after-lunch slump.

"I encourage you to go into the woods around us, walk slowly and mindfully, and pay attention to your thoughts, your breath, and the nature around you. This is intended to be a contemplative exercise. And please, no talking allowed."

We all rose to our feet and headed the door, scattering into different directions. I didn't have to turn around to know that Elizabeth was walking behind me. I could feel her presence. We walked about a quarter of a mile before I finally turned to confront her.

"This is supposed to a be a solitary meditation," I snipped.

She raised a finger to her lips. "Shhh. No talking."

Rolling my eyes at her, I turned around and stalked away, traveling deeper into the woods. I was supposed to be enjoying nature and letting my mind focus on my breath, instead I was engaging in a running internal monologue about the woman who was still following a step behind me.

We came to a clearing where one of the many mountain-fed streams ran through the woods. A wooden foot bridge ran across it. Elizabeth grabbed my hand and led me up a path to some large flat rocks alongside the river, a little ways away from the bridge. I don't know why, but I followed along, maybe because I was curious what she would do next.

We sat side by side on the rocks, staring at the rushing water of the river below us for several minutes until Elizabeth finally turned to me, her face vulnerable.

"I want to say that I'm sorry Miranda. I'm sorry that I hurt you with my behavior. I acted egregiously." Her voice was soft and sincere.

"You've always been my biggest regret. I was a coward, and we both paid the price for it. But I'm not the same scared little girl I was in college, not anymore. Please, can we at least be friends again?"

I held up my finger to my lips and repeated her instructions from earlier. "Shhh. No talking."

My hand moved up to tangle in the thick waves of her hair. We both moved forward at the same time and our lips met in a frantic kiss. Fire immediately raced through my veins. Our tongues tangled and our hands explored. I didn't know what I was doing exactly, I only knew that I was going to die if I didn't come soon.

It had been a long time since I'd dated anyone, but that didn't explain my instant and intense state of arousal. That was all Elizabeth. I pulled back and stared at her face. Her blue and lavender eyes were huge against the paleness of her face. I kicked off my boots and waved my hand between us.

"Make me come. Now."

Her eyes widened at my order, but she didn't hesitate. Within ten seconds I was flat on my back with my pants and underwear tossed to the side. I was dimly aware that we were just off the hiking path where anyone could come by, but couldn't bring myself to care. Sagebrush was very much about body love and "live and let live" so if there was any place we could safely fuck in public, this was it.

Elizabeth crawled between my legs, much as she'd done that night long ago, and began licking my pussy like her life depended on. Up and down, her tongue laved my slit. I felt her slide her tongue into my channel, fucking me with her tongue, and I moaned loudly.

She pulled away. "Shhh."

I grabbed her hair, tugging at the strands. After just one kiss, I was already needy and desperate.

"For fuck's sake, get on with it."

Her fingers invaded my channel, first one then two, pushing in and out, curving as she sought out my G-spot. Meanwhile her tongue roughly circled my clit until I was writing beneath her, mindlessly whispering things that might have been words, I don't know for sure.

Good lord, she'd really improved her technique over the last fifteen years. The woman really knew her way around a pussy.

My mouth opened in a silent scream as my orgasm rocked through my body. I'd never come so hard or so quickly in my life, at least not without my trusty Magic Wand vibrator. Pure pleasure flooded my entire body as it quaked and trembled under Elizabeth's talented mouth and fingers.

When it finally stopped I just lay there on the rocks, staring at the blue sky while I tried to catch my breath.

Elizabeth rolled over onto her side next to me, her head propped up one hand. Her expression was pure satisfaction. "Enjoyed that, did we?"

I surged up to a seated position and grabbed her under the arms, pulling her across me and arranging her face down over my lap.

She squeaked in shock. "What are you doing?"

"You've been a very bad girl, Elizabeth."

Elizabeth

If I hadn't already been completely turned on after pleasuring Miranda, the way she manhandled me across her lap would have done it. I was extremely glad that I'd foregone pants today when I felt her draw my broomstick skirt up to my waist. She tugged my panties down to my knees and before I could take a breath Miranda's hand came down on my bare ass.

Thwack!

I gasped in surprise as pain bloomed across my butt cheek, then faded to pleasure. I'd never been spanked before, and clearly I'd been missing something good. It felt incredible.

Thwack!

Thwack!

I stayed silent as Miranda worked out her emotions on my rear end. I could feel the heat rising in my skin as she continued to punish me. I didn't need to ask why. I deserved her punishment as much as she deserved to administer it.

Thwack!

Thwack!

The pain increased, and to my shock I felt tears rise up. I wasn't one to cry normally, but the pain and pleasure and humiliation of being spanked like a child combined to release emotions I didn't even know I had. It was cathartic.

The negative emotions ebbed as quickly as they had arisen, leaving me hot and bothered. I was incredibly turned on, and I found myself lifting my ass, meeting her stroke for stroke.

Eventually Miranda ran out of steam. She stroked my throbbing ass with her hand, soothing me, then slipped her fingers lower. I separated my legs to give her access, and she slid her fingers into my dripping slit.

"Enjoyed that, did we?" Once again she repeated my own words back to me.

"Please," I gasped. "Please!"

I wanted to come so bad I was shaking.

Fortunately, Miranda didn't punish me anymore. She slipped two fingers into my channel and began moving roughly in and out while I shamelessly humped her hand.

She reached down and pinched my nipple. Even through my light sweater and bra it felt sharp, sending a jolt right down to my core.

"Ahh!" I moaned. "Fuck!"

She pinched me again as she continued pumping her fingers in and out of my channel. I was so wet I could hear her fingers moving through my arousal.

"I'm so close," I whispered. I couldn't believe it was happening so fast, but I could already feel my pussy spasming.

Her hand lifted away from my breasts and moved up to my neck. Miranda wrapped her palm around my neck, squeezing with just enough pressure to dominate me, not enough to cut off my breath. The combination of the hand on my neck, the burning pain in my ass, and her talented fingers pumping in and out of me coalesced until I gasped her name and came with a long moan of pleasure.

My toes curled and I thrashed around on her lap as the force of my orgasm took over my body, leaving me feeling boneless and totally spent. I lay there across Miranda's lap for several long moments before pushing myself up to my knees. Miranda and stared at each other, then she gave me a long, sweet kiss.

"Don't fuck up again."

She pulled on her pants and underwear and slid into her boots while I remained kneeling, staring at her. She clearly wasn't angry anymore, but I could sense a wariness coming over her.

Miranda glanced at her sports watch. "Time to head back."

She took my hand in hers and pulled me to standing. I rearranged my skirt and pulled my underwear up, feeling a bit uncertain about what this all meant. I'd started this, that was for sure, but I couldn't interpret Miranda's expression right now.

Was this just a 'get back at Elizabeth' thing? Had she forgiven me? I'd just had one of the most incredible experiences of my life with her. Where did we go next?

I was too emotionally exhausted to talk, but I felt heartened when she let me thread my fingers through hers, which I took as a good sign. We walked back to the lodge in total silence, each lost in our own thoughts.

We rejoined our group and participated in a discussion about the role of nature in spirituality and some other activities, then we broke for dinner. Miranda and I ate with a few other women from our retreat, sitting side by side on the long wooden benches as we all enjoyed a hearty dinner that included whole grains, fresh vegetables, and honey-sweetened desserts.

We were just finishing up when one of the retreat leaders came over to our table. "Are you ready to get started, Elizabeth?"

I saw Miranda's curious look.

"I'm doing tarot readings tonight."

I knew the organizers of this event. They were part of the New Age community in Seattle, and they'd offered me a reduced price on the retreat in exchange for working three hours on

Saturday night doing tarot card readings for the other participants.

"Oh, OK." Miranda looked disappointed for an instant before she schooled her expression. "I guess I'll see you tomorrow then."

I leaned forward. "How about a late night soak after I finish with my session?" I suggested. "I haven't been in the pools yet and I've been dying to go."

Sagebrush was well known for its therapeutic hot springs. I'd been meaning to go last night but after my run-in with Miranda in front of her cabin I'd been too distracted to go.

"Yeah, sure."

It wasn't the enthusiastic response I'd been hoping for, but I could see that Miranda had gone into self-protection mode. It actually gave me a lot of hope. If she was trying to guard herself from having her heart broken again, clearly her heart was involved as much as mine was. I just needed to be patient.

I leaned forward and kissed her right on the lips. "I'll pick you up at nine."

Miranda

Elizabeth knocked on my cabin door a few minutes after nine o'clock. It was a cool, clear night, and the moon was full and bright in the sky. I forced myself to walk slowly to the door, not wanting to appear too eager.

My college crush stood on my porch holding a flashlight under her chin, aimed at her face, making it glow eerily like kids did when they told ghost stories.

"The call was coming from inside the house," she intoned in a spooky voice, imitating a horror movie we'd watched together several times.

I laughed, which was surely her intention. I'd forgotten how much I'd laughed back when I was friends with Elizabeth. She had a quirky sense of humor that somehow played off of my much drier humor.

She held out an elbow for me to grab. We walked arm in arm as we headed down to one of the main pool areas. It was about a seven minute walk away from the cabins. The path was still dim, despite the fullness of the moon, and Elizabeth used her flashlight to highlight the path.

We passed a couple of people coming back the other direction, probably on a private retreat. The light of the flashlight shone on the couple, making it clear that they were naked except for their flip flops.

"Jesus Christ, you can't swing a flashlight without hitting a naked dick around here," I groused.

Elizabeth laughed. "I guess he's not here for the lesbian retreat."

We walked farther into the woods, sticking to the well-worn paths that led to the pool areas. The first two pools had people in them, and although they invited us to join them, we both wanted to be alone.

We stuck paydirt on the third pool. It was small, surrounded by smooth river stones, and we quickly took off our robes and slid into the water. Pretty much no one wore swimsuits since the pool area was "clothing optional".

We slid into the warm bubbly water. Steam rose off the surface, and we sat down on the built-in benches, submerging ourselves up to our shoulders. As we soaked away our aches and pains, Elizabeth and I talked, really talked, for the first time since that fateful night in college.

Fifteen years was a lot to catch up on. I told her how hard it was to go through my last year at University of San Francisco without her. I told her about how my mom got cancer and died right after I graduated, and how my father later remarried to woman who was only ten years old than us, but really nice. And I told her about my life in Portland and my work at the homeless youth center.

"A high percentage of the homeless youth population identifies as LGBTQ," I told her.

"Really? Why?"

"They don't feel accepted at home, or they get kicked out of their foster care placements. It's not just a Portland problem, that's true of all the youth programs across the country. Even now, there are a lot of families who aren't very open to having kids with a different sexual orientation."

Saying it out loud reminded me of how bad it would have been for Elizabeth if she'd come out to her parents all those years ago. I'd never really considered how risky it would have been for her. Her thoughts clearly were going in the same direction as mine.

"Wow, that would have been me if I had come out to my parents when I was a teenager instead of waiting until I was thirty," she said. "I probably would have wound up on the streets too."

"Have you talked to them since you came out to them?"

She shook her head and her eyes filled with tears. "I don't know if they were more upset about me divorcing Michael or being a lesbian. Either one of those likely would have gotten me disowned, but both together? No way."

I reached under the bubbles and found her hand, squeezing her fingers softly as she continued.

"My mother collapsed on the floor sobbing like a huge tragedy had befallen her. My father flew into a rage. I'll never forget the way he got into my face, screaming and so angry that he had spittle in the corner of his lips. He told me he forbid me from being a lesbian. I burst out laughing. I couldn't help it. I was thirty years old at the time, for God's sake."

"Then what happened?"

"He pulled out what I was sure he thought was his trump card. He threatened to cut me off financially, which was funny really because they hadn't given me any financial support since I left college anyway. I reminded him of that and then he said they were going to dissolve the trust fund they'd set up for me to inherit when they died. I told him to go right ahead, because I didn't want their money if it came with strings," she said proudly.

"I walked out of there with my head held high. A few days later a courier delivered legal papers telling me I was disowned. I wrote 'fuck off' across the top and sent them back."

I laughed.

"When my divorce was final, Michael and I sold the house and split up all the assets. I had a couple friends up there, so I loaded up my car and moved to Seattle to start a new life on my own terms."

"Do you like living in Seattle?" I asked curiously. "I go up there every few years, but I haven't really formed an opinion."

"Yeah, I love it. I have good friends and an adorable little house on Bainbridge Island."

"Fancy," I noted. I wasn't super familiar with Seattle, but I knew that was one of the more wealthy parts of the city.

"You know how it is. The houses in California are all a bazillion dollars, so even though I bought a house in a relatively expensive area, I had a lot more purchasing power in Washington compared to California," she explained. "It's a great two bedroom cottage on a huge lot backing up to a natural area. In the morning I'll often see deer or other wildlife wandering through the backyard."

"It sounds great." I had never purchased a house. The prices were too expensive in Portland, at least for someone living on a non-profit salary.

"It is. I can't wait for you to see it."

Her comment reminded me that we lived one hundred and fifty miles apart. On a good day that was more than three hours away given the traffic on I-5. Suddenly I felt exhausted. I rose to sit on the edge of the pool, my heart suddenly heavy.

"This hot water is making me tired," I told her. "I'm going to head back to my cabin."

Elizabeth's head cocked to the side, and I knew she was trying to figure out the reason for my sudden change of mood.

"Hold on, I'll go with you."

She climbed out of the pool, and I couldn't help but stare at her. With her generous curves and pale white skin, she shimmered like a goddess in the moonlight. Elizabeth cleared her throat, letting me know that she'd noticed me staring at her.

"Can you hand me my robe please?" She gestured at the bench next to me.

I picked up the robe and walked over to her, reaching around to drape it over her shoulders. Keeping my grip on her robe, I used to drag her forward until she was pressed against me. The robe dropped as I slid my fingers into her hair and kissed her until we were both breathless.

When I'd gotten out of the pool, I'd convinced myself that I needed to get away from her. I told myself I'd go back to my cabin and try to minimize contact with her tomorrow so it would hurt less when we parted.

But kissing her under the moonlight, I made a different decision. The retreat was ending tomorrow, and we lived three hours apart. Chances were good I could only have tonight. I knew I was probably making a bad decision, but even if we could only have one night together, I still wanted it. Maybe one night would be enough.

"Come to my cabin," I whispered against her lips. "Spend the night with me."

Her eyes were searching. "Are you sure?"

I gave her a coy smile. "More sure than I've been about anything."

Elizabeth

I woke up surrounded by Miranda. I was shorter than her and ended up being the "little spoon" when we cuddled last night. Nothing made me happier than to come awake and feel her chin at the top of my head, the front of her body pressed along my naked back, and her arms and legs looped over me, holding me close. I hoped this was exactly how I'd wake up from now on. I wanted forever with her.

As comfortable as I was, I had some urgent needs to address. I carefully slipped out of bed, moving slowly to avoid waking Miranda up. I grabbed my robe, and tiptoed out the door, closing the door quietly behind me. Fortunately, Miranda's cabin was not too far from the bathhouse, because my bladder was screaming at me.

After I peed I took a few minutes to wash my face and brush my teeth. I'd left my toiletries in a caddy on the shelves in the bathhouse. Feeling refreshed, I stopped at my cabin to change my clothes and get ready for our last retreat day. On my way out, I grabbed my cold brew coffee pot and two travel mugs, and then headed back up to Miranda's cabin.

I could hear her talking to herself through the door. She sounded angry. I wondered what could have possibly happened? She'd been sleeping so peacefully when I'd left twenty minutes ago.

"I brought coffee!" I announced cheerfully as I swung her door open. The cabins didn't lock, and this far up into the mountains they didn't need to.

Miranda stiffened, stopped pacing, and turned slowly around to face me. I couldn't discern her expression, it looked like a combination of panic, anger, and relief.

"You came back?" she asked, blinking like she thought I was a mirage.

I frowned. "Why wouldn't I?"

Then it hit me. Miranda had woken up and thought I'd ditched her after one night together, the same way I'd done all those years ago. Silly woman.

I set the coffee and cups on the desk and walked slowly towards her. Setting one hand on either shoulder, I looked her straight in the eye.

"I. Will. Always. Come. Back. To you."

It was a promise, and we both knew it. This wasn't just some weekend fling. I could see the realization in her eyes.

I leaned forward and kissed her, my tongue tangling with hers. Without breaking contact, I walked us backwards towards the bed. When the back of my knees hit the mattress I pulled away, flopping down on my back, and crooking my finger at her.

"Up here. Now."

She glanced at her smart watch. "We only have twenty minutes before morning meditation."

"Then you'd better get moving. I want you to sit on my face."

Her dark brown eyes darkened. "Yes ma'am."

Miranda threw off her robe and crawled up the bed on her hands and knees. Her progress was excruciatingly slow as she stopped to give my pussy several long licks, then kissed her way up my torso and across my breasts. When she got close enough, I grabbed her hips and pulled her down over my face. Miranda laughed, and grabbed onto the metal headboard above my head.

I brought her down and began licking up and down her folds, stopping to tap and suck at her clit before starting over again. Her pussy was a pinkish brown color, neatly trimmed, and I swear it tasted better than any other pussy I'd sampled. And believe me when I say that I'd sampled quite a few.

I might not have come out until I was thirty, but I'd done quite a bit of making up for lost time over the past five years. Seattle was crawling with lesbians. All that was irrelevant now, of course. Miranda had been my first, and now she would be my last.

In less than five minutes she was writhing above me and making little whining noises. I held on tight to her hips, keeping her in place while I ravished her with my tongue.

She stiffened then shuddered as her orgasm overtook her. "Elizabeth! Fuck!"

Her sweet nectar flooded my mouth and I licked it up eagerly while she came down from her orgasm.

"Fuck," she said again as she slid off me and rolled onto her side. I put my arm around her and cuddled her in close.

"Just give me a few minutes to recover, then I'll take care of you," she said sleepily.

"No," I told her. "This was about you. And besides, I got a lot of enjoyment out of feeling you come on my face."

She rolled her eyes, then looked at her watch again. "Oh crap, we have to get down to the lodge."

She got out of bed and pulled on some underwear, yoga pants and a long-sleeved t-shirt. I poured us each a cup of coffee to drink on the way down.

"You ready to go?" I asked.

Miranda nodded and we headed out. It was a beautiful, sunny day and I felt lighter and happier than I had in years. I glanced over at her as we walked down the path. Her eyes were shadowed, and she looked pensive.

"What's going on in that brain of yours?" I asked.

"Nothing. Just remembering that today is our last day here."

The retreat lasted until noon, then we were able to have a final lunch if we chose to before heading home.

I nudged her with my shoulder and gave her a smile. "Let's focus on our morning session, then we can talk about the future over lunch."

Miranda gave me a big smile. "So, there's a future?"

"You bet your ass there is. I intend to spend the rest of my life with you."

She gave me a sweet smile. "Coincidentally, I have the exact same plans."

Epilogue—Miranda

Two years later...

"Ahhh! Fuck. Shit. Damn!"

I winced as my wife gripped my hand and swore like a sailor. "Why the FUCK did I let you talk me into this?"

"You lost the coin toss, remember?"

Elizabeth glared at me. Usually she was the sweeter personality between us, but childbirth was clearly bringing out her bad side.

Right after our retreat weekend I'd quit my job and moved up to Seattle to live with Elizabeth. She had offered to move to Portland instead, but the truth was I was burned out at my job and knew I could easily find a new one at any of the myriad of social service agencies in Seattle. And I did. The last two years I'd been working as a hospital social worker, making almost twice as much as I had in Portland.

Elizabeth's house on Bainbridge Island was awesome. I didn't really have a lot of belongings, having always worked in the low-paying world of social services, but the things I did bring soon were incorporated into the space. With some painting and redecorating, we'd made it our own, working together.

On the six month anniversary of us running into each other at the retreat center, or "our first date", as Elizabeth referred to it, she proposed to me.

We married a few weeks later. It was just a simple courthouse ceremony with my dad and stepmother and our close friends. After much consideration, we'd sent an invitation to Elizabeth's parents, but they never responded. I couldn't say I was surprised

– neither of us were – but putting out the olive branch had seemed like the right thing to do.

After a year together we decided we were ready to have children. After investigating all the options, we decided to go with IVF and a sperm donor. I wasn't joking, we'd flipped a coin to determine who would carry the baby. And that's how Elizabeth wound up in a delivery room, swearing and screaming as we waited for our daughter to make her debut.

An hour later it was all over. I cradled my wife in my arms, while she cradled little Nina. We'd named her for my mother. Nina was small and bald and red-faced and perfect. Perfectly ours. I'd never known how much I wanted a family until I looked down into that squishy little face.

I leaned down and kissed Nina's head, inhaling her sweet baby face, then I kissed Elizabeth on the cheek. She looked up at me with a smile. "I love you."

"I love you too, baby. Thanks for birthing us a baby."

Her expression turned stern. "You're going to carry the next one, damn it!"

***

If you liked this book, please consider leave a review or rating on my author page to let me know.

Want a free book? Join my newsletter and receive a free copy of my book "Hotel Spanking" for free. Be the first to hear about new releases and sales. Click here[1] and download your free book today.

---

1.   *https://bit.ly/rebabooks*

Be sure to keep reading for a free preview from Reba Bale's "Divorce Recovery" series, available now on all major retailers.

Special Preview

Spanking Justice: A Middle-Aged Divorcee's First Spanking
The Divorce Recovery Team Series
Book 1
By Reba Bale

"Congratulations Amy, you're officially divorced."

Mark Winston, her divorce attorney, slid the folder of papers across the heavy wooden desk. Amy leaned forward hesitantly and placed her hand on the folder without picking it up. She could still see a faint tan line where her wedding ring used to be.

She bit her lip and sighed. "Thanks. I guess."

"What is it?" Mark asked, his deep voice causing a shiver down her spine. "Most people are relieved when the process is finally completed. You're free to move forward with your life now, like your ex-husband will do."

Amy nodded. "I know. I hope that feeling of relief will come later. It's just..."

"Just what?" Mark asked, tipping his head to the side curiously.

Amy studied him for a moment. He really was a handsome man. She estimated his age to be early fifties, about ten years older than she was. She had turned forty a few months ago. His hair was dark and thick, with silver highlights near his temples giving him a distinguished air. Small lines bracketed his mouth as he gave her a small encouraging smile. Something about him made her feel comfortable to confide in him.

"I can't help but think about all the things I did wrong in the relationship," she said, her voice small. "If I knew now what I know then, would I have done some things differently to save the relationship."

Mark looked at her intently. "You gave almost twenty years to your marriage Amy. You put your own career on the back burner to raise your son. You kept the house. And then your husband decided to move on to someone younger. It's a pretty typical story, honestly."

"I know," she nodded. "But I've been thinking of all the times I nagged, all the times I was too tired from running around with my son to take care of myself, all the times I said no to sex or date night. John cheated and there's absolutely no excuse for that. But I realize at some point I gave up on the marriage too. I'm having a hard time forgiving myself for the things I did, or didn't do, to keep the relationship alive."

Mark looked at her thoughtfully. "You'll need to forgive yourself in order to move on," he said. "Otherwise, you'll just stagnate and think about the past. You do want to move on, don't you?"

Amy nodded again. "Yes, of course. I just need to stop beating myself up."

Mark steepled his hands on the desk and stared at her intently until she met his gaze for the first time since she walked into the office. His eyes were serious. "What if I told you that we have a way to help you move on? A service that has helped so many women like yourselves recover from their divorces and go on to have a happy life."

She looked at him curiously. "How? What do you mean?"

"Our firm offers a unique service for people like you. People who want to, shall we say, accept the consequences of their own part in the demise of their marriage. We will punish you for your actions, then you can move on. We give you absolution of a sorts. Then you are able to forgive yourself too."

"Punish me? Like what, a spanking?" she laughed, ignoring the small thrill in her belly when she said it.

Mark's eyes sparked as if he knew what she was thinking. "Yes, that's exactly right. We call it our Divorce Discipline package. You agree to be spanked or punished by us for everything you did wrong, then it's over and you can move on."

"You're offering to spank me?" she squeaked.

"That's exactly what I'm offering you. It's safe, confidential and quite therapeutic," he said, pulling an envelope out of his drawer.

"I know it's a lot to think about so take some time. Here's the contract for our Divorce Discipline package. Read it over, and if you decide you want to move forward, call my assistant, and tell her you want a DD appointment with me after hours. I'll handle your case myself."

"Is this a joke?" she asked, looking around for a hidden camera.

For more of the story, check out "Spanking Justice" by Reba Bale, available for immediate download on your favorite retail sites today.

***

Want a free book? Join my newsletter and receive a free copy of my book "Hotel Spanking" for free. I promise I will only email you when there are new releases or special sales, so click here[1] and sign up today.

---

1. *https://bit.ly/rebabooks*

Other Books by Reba Bale

Check out my other books, available on most major online retailers now:

Punishing Holidays

Turkey and a Spanking

Shopping and a Spanking

Unlikely Doms Series

Alpha in a Sweater Vest

Alpha Plumber

Hotel Spanking

Alpha Student

Alpha Yogi

The Voyeur Romance Series

Naughty Sunbathing

Naughty Dinner Date

Naughty Laundry Date

Naughty Camping

The Spanking Therapy Series

The Reluctant Bride's First Spanking

The Reluctant Bride Gets Caught

The Billionaire Gets Punished

The Divorce Recovery Series

Spanking Justice: A Middle-Aged Divorcee's First Spanking

A Punishing Workout: Spanked by the Trainer

A Disciplined Budget: Spanked by the Accountant

The Curvy Reporter Gets Punished

Paying for Tuition

The Babysitter's Ride Home

The Babysitter's First Menage

The Teaching Assistant's Lesson

The Billionaire's Assistant

The Marriage Survival Series

Finding His Alpha: A Wife's First Spanking

Watching His Wife: The First Time Sharing

Exploring His Fantasy: A First Time Gay Ménage

Toys for Grown-Ups Series

Financial Punishment

Menage a Geek

Sharing with Strangers Series

Night Train

The Ride of My Life

Friends to Lovers Series

The Divorcee's First Time: A Lesbian Romance

My BFF's Sister: A Hot Lesbian Romance

My Rockstar Assistant: A Hot Lesbian Romance

Standalones:

Share Me: A Cheating Husband's Punishment

Tornado Warning

Summer in Paradise

Want a free book? Join my newsletter and receive a free copy of my book "Hotel Spanking" for free. I promise I will only email you when there are new releases or special sales, so click here[1] and sign up today.

---

1. *https://bit.ly/rebabooks*

About the Author

Reba Bale loves writing naughty stories where the characters are able to tap into their inner fantasies and experience spanking, bondage, humiliation, or other activities on the non-vanilla side of life. When Reba is not writing she is reading the same naughty stories she likes to write.

Be sure to follow Reba on your favorite retailer and sign up for her newsletter so you are first to hear about all the new releases. Click here to join Reba's newsletter mailing list.[2]

---

2.   https://bit.ly/rebabooks

Don't miss out!

Visit the website below and you can sign up to receive emails whenever Reba Bale publishes a new book. There's no charge and no obligation.

https://books2read.com/r/B-A-IDTM-MKMWB

BOOKS 2 READ

Connecting independent readers to independent writers.

Did you love *My College Crush*? Then you should read *The Divorcee's First Time: A Hot Friends-to-Lovers Lesbian Romance*[3] by Reba Bale!

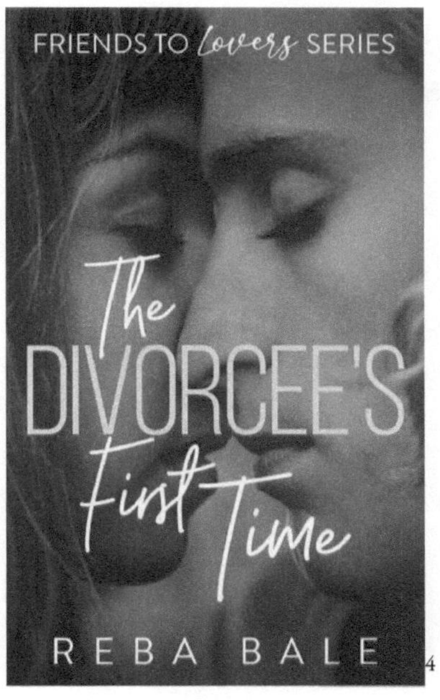

When Jennifer goes out with her best friend Susan to celebrate her divorce, she gets more than she bargained for. The dominant older woman gives Jennifer her first time lesbian experience and changes things forever. Will it be a one-time thing, or will their hot and steamy night lead to more? This friends to lovers novella is standalone romance intended for adult audiences only, due to explicit scenes and light BDSM.

---

3. https://books2read.com/u/bpznKX

4. https://books2read.com/u/bpznKX